RH

The Water Dragon

A Chinese Legend

Copyright © 2012 Shanghai Press and Publishing Development Company
All rights reserved. Unauthorized reproduction, in any manner, is prohibited.
This book is edited and designed by the Editorial Committee of *Cultural China* series

Managing Directors: Wang Youbu, Xu Naiqing
Editorial Director: Wu Ying
Editors: Yang Xiaohe, Ginley Regencia

Story and Illustrations: Li Jian
Translation: Yijin Wert

ISBN: 978-1-60220-978-7

Address any comments about *The Water Dragon* to:

Better Link Press
99 Park Ave
New York, NY 10016
USA
or
Shanghai Press and Publishing Development Company
F 7 Donghu Road, Shanghai, China (200031)
Email: comments_betterlinkpress@hotmail.com

Printed in China by Shenzhen Donnelley Printing Co., Ltd.

3   5   7   9   10   8   6   4   2

The Water Dragon

A Chinese Legend

Retold in English and Chinese

By Li Jian

Better Link Press

Long long ago in China, a little boy named Ah Bao lived in a small mountain village. Every day, Ah Bao went into the forest to collect wood.

很久以前在中国的一个小山村里，住着一个叫阿宝的孩子，他每天都要到山中打柴。

One day, as he gathered wood, Ah Bao saw a shiny red stone lying in the grass. He picked it up, wondering what it could be.

一天打柴的时候，阿宝看到草丛里有一颗珠子，红彤彤地发着光。他捡起了珠子，想知道这是什么东西。

Ah Bao put the shiny red stone in his rice crock. He immediately heard the rice rattling inside. Soon his crock was overflowing with rice. Ah Bao now had more rice than he could ever eat.

Ah Bao set the shiny red stone in his money jar. The coins inside the jar started rattling too. Soon the jar was overflowing with coins. Ah Bao now also had more money than he could ever spend.

The shiny red stone must be magical!

阿宝把珠子放在米缸里。他立刻听到米缸里传来哗啦哗啦的响声。不一会儿，米缸装满了，阿宝吃也吃不完。

阿宝把珠子放在钱罐里。他立刻听到钱罐传来哗啦哗啦的响声。不一会儿，钱罐装满了，阿宝花也花不完。

这原来是一颗有魔法的宝珠呀！

When his neighbors were out of rice, Ah Bao filled their rice crocks with the magic power of the red stone.

When his neighbors were out of money, Ah Bao gave them money made by the magic power of the red stone.

But ever since Ah Bao found the magic stone, it had stopped raining. In time, the rivers dried up and the crops died.

邻居家没米了，阿宝就用红宝珠的魔力把他们的米缸填满；

乡亲们没有钱花了，阿宝就用红宝珠的魔力把钱送给大家。

但是，自从阿宝捡到宝珠以后，天上就再也没有下过一滴雨。慢慢地，河水干涸了，再后来庄稼也枯死了。

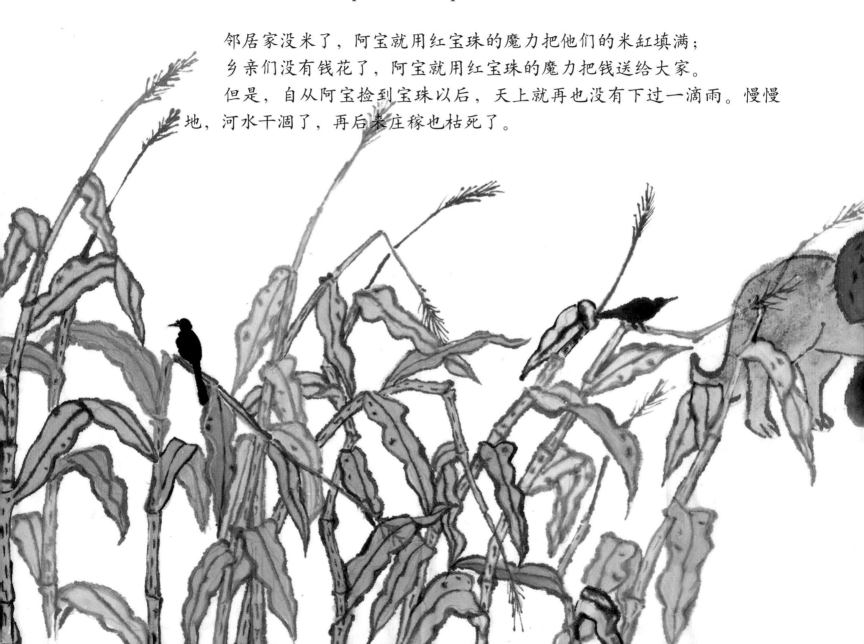

Ah Bao placed the magic stone in his water bucket, hoping it would overflow with water. To his surprise, the magic stone absorbed all the water in the bucket instead.

"How can we live without water?" he thought.

That night, Ah Bao dreamed of a white Water Dragon dancing in the clouds and showering the land with much needed water.

阿宝把宝珠放在水桶里，希望水能源源不断地流出来。奇怪的是，宝珠却吸光了桶里所有的水。

"没有水可怎么办呢？"他想。

那天晚上，阿宝做了一个梦：一条白色的雨龙飞舞在云雾里，雨水从它的嘴里喷涌而出洒向干涸的大地。

Early the next morning, Ah Bao decided to search for the Water Dragon. He packed food and the magic stone, then set off.

Some days later, Ah Bao met a giant snake blocking the road at the foot of a huge mountain.

"Do you know where I can find the Water Dragon?" Ah Bao asked.

"If you move the rock off my tail, I will tell you where he is," the snake replied.

第二天一早，阿宝决定去寻找那条雨龙。带上宝珠和干粮，他就出发了。

几天以后，他来到一座高山的山脚下，一条巨蛇挡住了他的道路。

"你知道雨龙在哪里吗？"阿宝问道。

"如果你帮我把尾巴上的石头搬走，我就告诉你！"巨蛇答道。

Ah Bao found a branch and lifted the rock off the snake's tail.

The giant snake gave Ah Bao a piece of his skin and said, "Boy, this will be very useful to you on your journey. The Water Dragon that you are looking for lives in the far east. Be careful, because you will meet a greedy red monster along the way."

　　阿宝找来一截树干，撬开了石头。

　　巨蛇送给阿宝一块蛇皮，说道："孩子，在旅途中你会用到它的。你要找的雨龙住在遥远的东方。路上你会遇到一只贪婪的红鬼，要小心它！"

Ah Bao thanked the giant snake for his snakeskin and continued his journey towards the east. He came to a nearly dry riverbed where he noticed a carp swimming in a pool of water.

"Do you know where I can find the Water Dragon?" Ah Bao asked.

"If you move me to the well over there, I will tell you where he is," the fish replied.

谢过巨蛇送他的蛇皮，阿宝向东出发了。他来到一条快要干涸的小河边，一条鲤鱼在水里游来游去。

"你知道雨龙在哪里吗？"阿宝问道。

"如果你把我捧到那边的井里，我就告诉你。"鲤鱼答道。

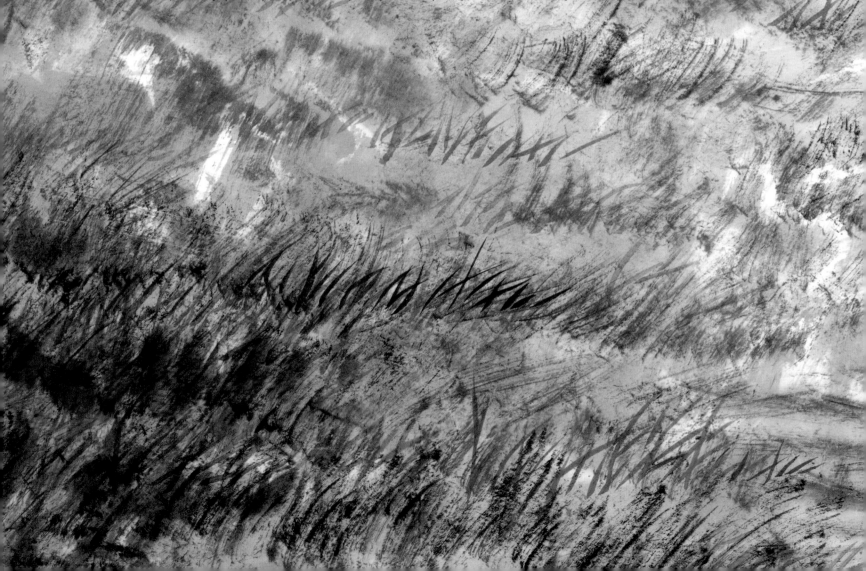

Ah Bao scooped the carp out of the river with both hands and placed him in the well.

The fish gave Ah Bao a piece of his skin with many scales on it and said, "Boy, this will be very useful to you on your journey. The Water Dragon that you are looking for lives in the far east. Be careful, because you will meet a greedy red monster along the way."

阿宝双手捧起鲤鱼，把它送到了水井里。

鲤鱼送给阿宝一片满是鱼鳞的鱼皮，说道："孩子，在旅途中你会用到它的。你要找的雨龙住在遥远的东方。路上你会遇到一只贪婪的红鬼，要小心它！"

Ah Bao thanked the fish for his scales and set off once again. Soon he was walking through a forest and came across a deer whose antlers were stuck in a tree.

"Do you know where I can find the Water Dragon?" Ah Bao asked.

"If you remove my antlers, I will tell you where he is," the deer replied.

　　谢过鲤鱼送他的鳞片，阿宝又出发了。不久以后，走过
一片树林时，他遇到了一只鹿角卡在树里的梅花鹿。

　　"你知道雨龙在哪里吗？"阿宝问道。

　　"如果你帮我砍掉鹿角，我就告诉你。"梅花鹿答道。

Ah Bao took his ax and cut the antlers from the deer.

The deer gave Ah Bao his antlers and said, "Boy, this will be very useful to you on your journey. The Water Dragon that you are looking for lives in the far east. Be careful, because you will meet a greedy red monster along the way."

阿宝用柴刀帮梅花鹿割掉了鹿角。

梅花鹿把他的角送给了阿宝，说道："孩子，在旅途中你会用到它的。你要找的雨龙在东方。路上你会遇到一只贪婪的红鬼，要小心它！"

Ah Bao thanked the deer for his antlers
and continued on his journey. Soon he came to a high cliff
where he met two eagles.

"Do you know where I can find the Water Dragon?" Ah Bao asked.

"If you can take my child to our nest at the top of the cliff, I will tell you where he is," an
eagle replied.

谢过梅花鹿送的鹿角，阿宝又上路了。不久，在一道悬崖下，他遇到两只苍鹰。

"你知道雨龙在哪里吗？"阿宝问道。

"如果你帮我把孩子送回悬崖顶上的巢里，我就告诉你！"一只苍鹰回答道。

Ah Bao climbed the cliff and laid the little eagle in his nest.

The eagle gave Ah Bao a pair of claws and said, "Boy, this will be very useful to you on your journey. The Water Dragon that you are looking for lives in the far east. Be careful, because you will meet a greedy red monster on your journey."

阿宝攀上悬崖，把小苍鹰放回他的巢里。

苍鹰送给阿宝一对利爪，说道："孩子，在旅途中你会用到它的。你要找的雨龙住在东方，路上你会遇到一只贪婪的红鬼，要小心它！"

Ah Bao thanked the eagles for the claws and continued his journey. It was not long before Ah Bao met the red monster that everyone had warned him about.

"Do you know where I can find the Water Dragon?" Ah Bao asked.

"You won't be able to find the dragon unless you have the dragon ball," the red monster replied sulkily.

"What does the dragon ball look like? Does it look like my red stone?" Ah Bao asked.

谢过苍鹰送的利爪，阿宝又上路了。不久，他果然遇到了那只大家都警告过他的红鬼。

"你知道雨龙在哪里吗？"阿宝问道。

"要想找到它，必须得有龙珠才行！"红鬼没好声气地答道。

"龙珠是什么样子的？像我的这颗珠子吗？"阿宝问道。

"Yes, that's it! You should not have it! Give it to me!" The greedy red monster jumped at Ah Bao to grab the dragon ball.

Knowing that he would not be able to defeat the monster, Ah Bao ran as fast as he could.

"I will eat you up if you run away!" The red monster shouted as he chased Ah Bao to the edge of the cliff.

"If I lose this dragon ball, I will never find the Water Dragon," Ah Bao thought to himself. He quickly swallowed the dragon ball and jumped off the cliff.

"哦，就是它，快把它给我，那不是你应该拥有的！"贪婪的红鬼扑向阿宝，来抢那颗龙珠。

阿宝知道自己打不过红鬼，只好拼命逃跑。

"你逃跑我就吃掉你！"红鬼大叫着，追着阿宝到了悬崖边。

"如果没有龙珠就找不到雨龙了！"阿宝对自己说。他飞快地吞下了龙珠，跳下了悬崖。

Ah Bao landed in a deep pool of water at the base
of the cliff…

阿宝掉在了悬崖下深深的潭水中……

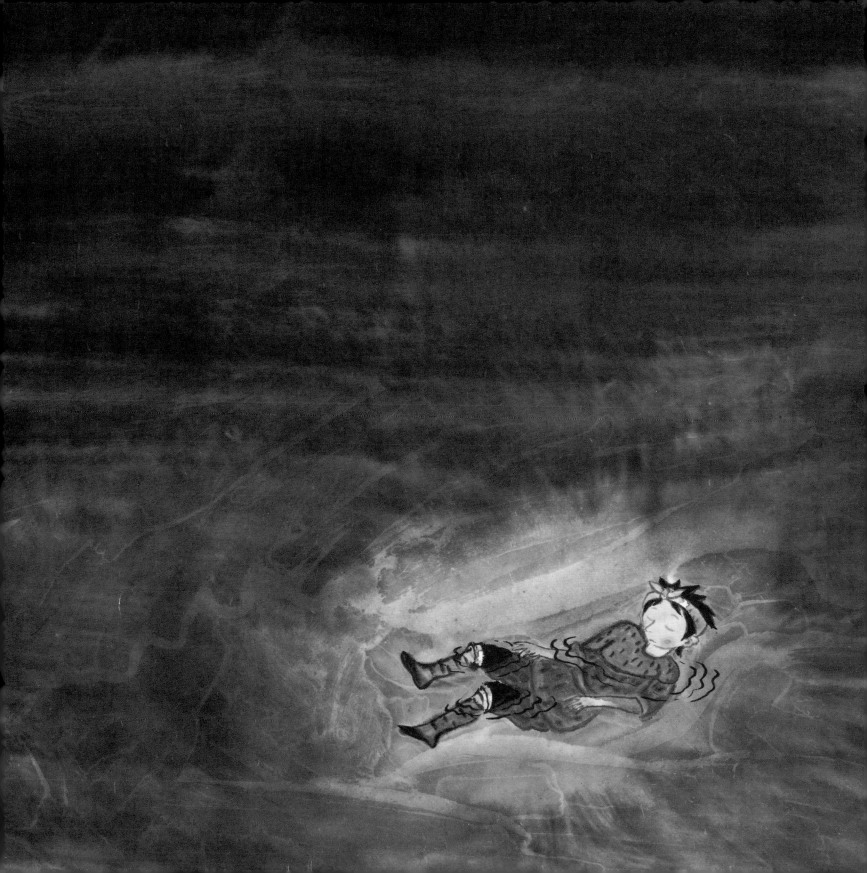

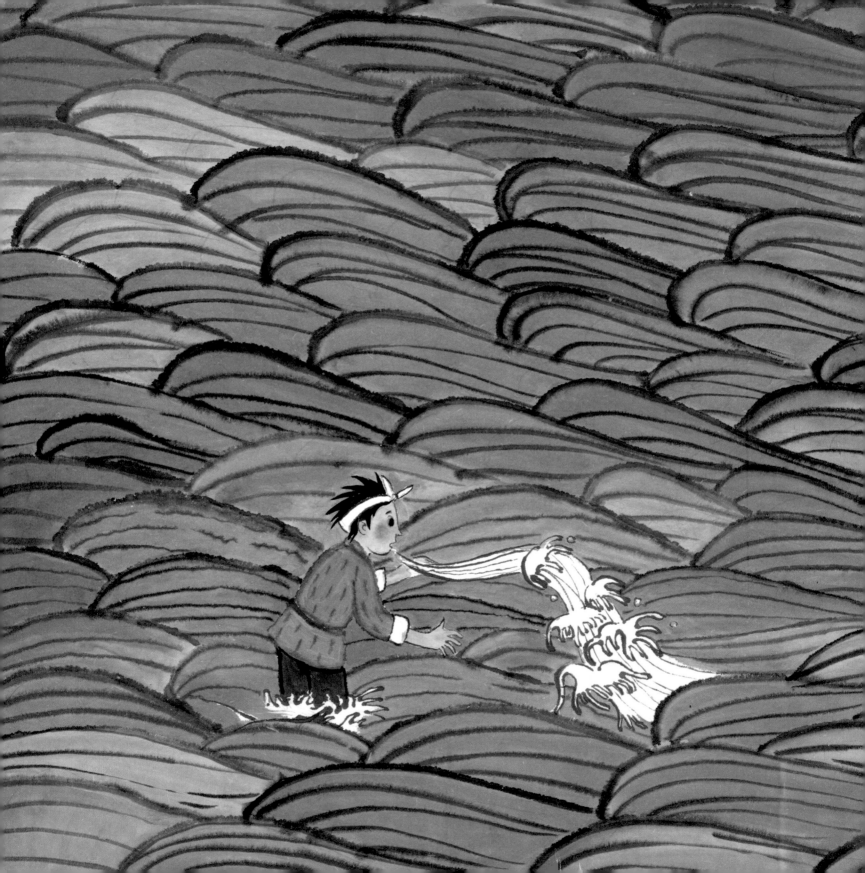

After swimming to shore, Ah Bao felt extremely thirsty. He started to drink from the pool of water and emptied it in seconds. Still, he was thirsty.

Ah Bao rushed to the East (China) Sea and started to drink the sea water. He kept drinking and drinking until his thirst was satisfied.

阿宝游到岸边，他觉得口渴极了，一口气喝干了潭水。他还是觉得很渴。

阿宝飞跑到东海边，喝起海水来！他喝呀喝呀……喝呀喝呀……终于没有那么渴了！

All of a sudden, Ah Bao's body was wrapped in the snakeskin. The deer's antlers attached to his head. The scales from the fish covered his back. His hands and feet were replaced by the claws from the eagles, and his eyes became red and shiny like the dragon ball.

突然，阿宝的身体裹上了蛇皮，他的头上长出了鹿角，他的背上覆盖了鱼鳞，他的手脚变成了鹰爪，他的眼睛变红了，像龙珠一样闪亮！

He flew into the sky, dancing in the clouds. Then he swooped down over the thirsty fields spraying water as he went. Ah Bao had turned into the Water Dragon!

他腾空而起，飞舞在云彩中。水从他的嘴里喷涌而出，化成清雨洒向干渴的大地！
原来阿宝变成了那条雨龙！

The Water Dragon showered water on the dry earth until it turned green again.

That's the legend told of the kind Water Dragon, who was really just a little boy named Ah Bao.

雨龙遍洒雨水，干涸的大地又恢复了生机。

传说中，那条善良的雨龙就是阿宝那个孩子。